W9-AAT-645

HUDSON
PUBLIC LIBRARY

tiger tales
5 River Road, Suite 128, Wilton, CT 06897
Published in the United States 2013
Originally published in Great Britain 2013 by Little Tiger Press
 • ISBN-13: 978-1-58925-147-2/ISBN-10: 1-58925-147-4

For Finlay – my little star
C R

Printed in China • LTP/1800/0520/0513
10 9 8 7 6 5 4 3 2 1

Library of Congress Cataloging-in-Publication Data

Rayner, Catherine, author, illustrator.
Abigail / by Catherine Rayner.
pages cm
Summary: Abigail the giraffe wants to count the spots and stripes on her animal friends, Ladybug, Zebra, and Cheetah, but when they move too fast for counting, Abigail comes up with a new plan.
ISBN 978-1-58925-147-2 (hardcover) — ISBN 1-58925-147-4 (hardcover) [1. Counting — Fiction. 2. Giraffe — Fiction. 3. Animals — Fiction.] I. Title.
PZ7.R2297Ab 2013
[E] — dc23

2013009088

by Catherine Rayner

Abigail

tiger tales®

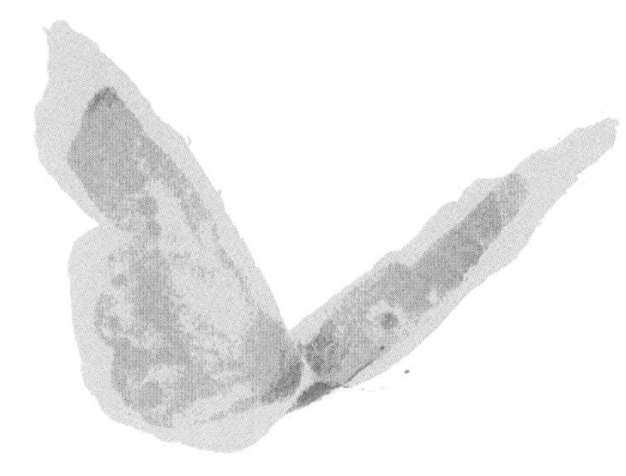

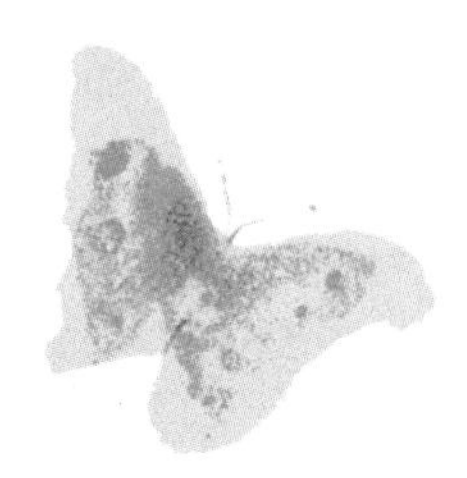

Abigail *loved* to count.
It was her very favorite thing.

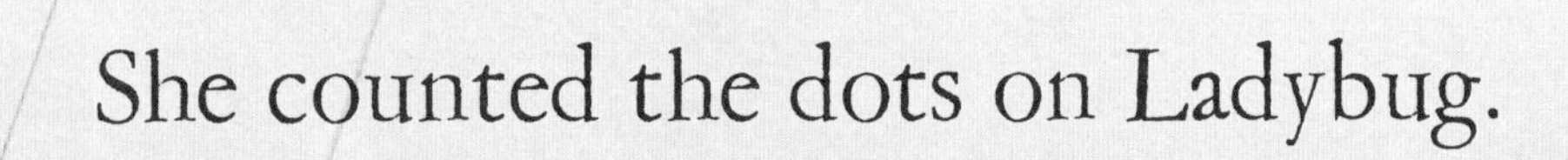

She counted the dots on Ladybug.

1

2

3

But Ladybug scurried
under a leaf.

So Abigail counted the leaves
on the tree.

BUT . . .

. . . somebody was eating the leaves!

Crunch!

Munch!

Lunch!

Abigail *really* wanted to count.

She started counting Zebra's stripes.

7
8
9

“It’s INCREDIBLY difficult to count when you are moving, Zebra,” grumbled Abigail.

But Zebra just couldn’t help it.

And there was no point even *trying* to count Cheetah's splotches.

Whoosh . . . .

He was just too fast.

“Come **back**, everybody!” said Abigail, crossly.

"Oh, dear," sighed Abigail. "There must be *something* I can count."

"I know just the thing,"

whispered Ladybug.

"Follow me."

“FLOWERS!” giggled Zebra. “Come on – we’ll help you count!”
Unfortunately, Abigail’s friends were not very good at counting.

"One . . . two . . . six . . . lots!" bellowed Zebra.

"One . . . three . . . five . . . many!" laughed Cheetah.

It was impossible!

But Abigail was a very patient giraffe.
Carefully, she showed her friends
how to count.

1

2

3

4

5

6 7 8 9 10

They practiced all day long until at
last their counting was nearly perfect.
But by that time . . .

. . . it was dark.

"Oh, no!" grunted Zebra. "How can we count when the sun has set?"

Cheetah's tail drooped, and Ladybug frowned.

But Abigail just smiled.
"Don't give up, everyone . . . ."

“Look!”

High above, the stars were twinkling, and they were not going anywhere . . . .

Together, Abigail and her friends counted all night long.

3 friends. **1,267** stars.

And **1** Abigail.